SHORT STORIES
BY

Munshi Premchand

First published in India in 2018

ISBN: 978-93-88333-04-7

Invincible Publishers
G-120, Sushant Lok III, Sector 57, Gurgaon-122002

Registered Address: Opposite Kasturba Ashram,
Radaur, Haryana – 135133

List of Stories

IDGAAH

THE FESTIVAL OF EID

A full thirty days after Ramadan comes Eid. How wonderful and beautiful is the morning of Eid! The trees look greener, the fields more festive, the sky has a lovely pink glow. The sun comes up brighter and more dazzling than before to wish the world a very happy Eid. The village is agog with excitement. Everyone is up early to go to the Eidgaah mosque. It is a good three miles from the village. There will be hundreds of people to greet and chat with; they would certainly not be finished before midday.

The boys are more excited than the others. Some of them kept only one fast— and that too only till noon. Some didn't even do that. But no one can deny them the joy of going to the Eidgaah. Fasting is for the grown-ups and the aged. For the boys, it is only the day of Eid. They have been talking about it all the time. At long last the day has come. They have no concern with things that have to be done. They are not bothered whether or not there is enough milk and sugar for the 'kheer'. All they want is to eat the kheer.

Their pockets bulge with coins like the stomach of the pot-bellied Kubera, the Hindu God of Wealth. They are forever taking the treasure out of their pockets, counting and recounting it before putting it back. Mahmood counts, "One, two, ten, twelve"— he has twelve pice. Mohsin has "One, two, three, eight, nine, fifteen" pice. Out of this countless hoard, they will buy countless things: toys, sweets, paper-pipes, rubber balls— and much else.

The happiest of the boys is Hamid. He is only four; poorly dressed, thin and famished-looking. His parents are no more, but Hamid lives with Granny Ameena and is as happy as a lark. She tells him that his father has gone to earn money and will return with sack loads of silver. And that his mother has gone to Allah to get lovely gifts for him. This makes Hamid very happy. Hamid has no shoes on his feet; the cap on his head is soiled and tattered; its gold thread has turned black. Nevertheless, Hamid is happy. He knows that when his father comes back with sacks full of silver and his mother with gifts from Allah, he will be able to fulfil all his heart's desires. Then he will have more than Mahmood, Mohsin, Noorey and Sammi.

Hamid goes to his grandmother and says, "Granny, don't you fret over me! I will be the first to get back. Don't worry!"

Ameena frets over Hamid going away alone. Other boys are going out with their fathers, but she is the only 'father' Hamid has. What if he gets lost in the crowd? No, she must not lose her precious little soul! The only way out was to ask someone for them.

The villagers leave in one party. With the boys is Hamid. They reach the suburbs of the town. On both sides of the road are mansions of the rich enclosed all around by thick, high walls. Then come big buildings: the law courts, the college and the club.

They proceed to the stores of the sweet-meat vendors. All so gaily decorated! Every store has them piled up in mountain heaps.

"My Abba says that at midnight there is a Jinn at every stall. He has all that remains weighed and pays in real rupees, just the sort of rupees we have," says Mohsin.

Hamid is not convinced. "Where would the Jinns find all that money?"

"Jinns are never short of money," replies Mohsin. "They can get into any treasury they want. Mister, don't you know no iron bars can stop them? They are here one moment and five minutes later they can be in Calcutta."

It begins to get crowded. Parties heading for the Eidgaah are coming into town from different sides—

each one dressed better than the other. Some on tongas and ekkas, some in motorcars. All wearing perfume; all bursting with excitement.

For village children everything in the town is strange. Whatever catches their eye, they stand and gape at it with wonder. Cars hoot frantically to get them out of the way, but they couldn't care less. Hamid is nearly run over by a car.

At long last, the Eidgaah comes in view. Above it are massive tamarind trees casting their shade on the cemented floor on which carpets have been spread. And there are row upon row of worshippers as far as the eye can see, spilling well beyond the mosque courtyard. Newcomers line themselves behind the others. Here neither wealth nor status matters because in the eyes of Islam, all men are equal. Our villagers wash their hands and feet and make their own line behind the others. A hundred thousand heads bow together in prayer! And then all together they stand erect; bow down and sit on their knees!

Once the prayer gets over, men embrace each other. They all descend to the sweet and toy- vendors' stores outside like an army moving to an assault. There are swings and merry-go-rounds with animal shapes to mount on. Mahmood and Mohsin and Noorey and other boys pay one pice each to take twenty five rounds at the ride.

Hamid watches them from a distance. All he has are three pice. He couldn't afford to part with a third of his treasure so soon.

After the roundabouts, it is time for toys. There is a row of stalls on one side with all kinds of toys; soldiers and milkmaids, kings and ministers, water-carriers and washerwomen and holy men. Mahmood buys a policeman in khaki with a red turban on his head and a gun on his shoulder. It looks so lifelike, as if marching in a parade. Mohsin likes the water-carrier with his back bent under the weight of the water-bag. He holds the handle of the bag in one hand and looks pleased with himself. Noorey has fallen for the lawyer. A black gown over a long, white coat and a fat volume of some law book in his hand. It appears as if he has just finished arguing a case in a court of law.

These toys cost two pice each. All Hamid has are three pice; how can he afford to buy such expensive toys? If they dropped out of his hand, they would be smashed to bits. If a drop of water fell on them, the paint would run.

Mohsin says, "My water-carrier will sprinkle water every day, morning and evening."

Mahmood says, "My policeman will guard my house. If a thief comes near, he will shoot him with his gun.

Noorey says, "My lawyer will fight my cases."

Sammi says, "My washer-woman will wash my clothes every day."

Hamid dismisses them, but his eyes look at them hungrily and he wishes he could hold them in his hands for just a moment or two. But young boys are not givers, particularly when it is something new. Poor Hamid doesn't get to touch the toys.

After the toys come the sweets. Someone buys sesame seed candy, others gulab-jammuns or halva. They smack their lips with relish. Only Hamid is left out. He looks with hungry eyes at the others.

Mohsin says, "Hamid, take this sesame candy, it smells good."

Hamid suspects it is a cruel joke.

Hamid replies, "You keep your sweets. Don't I have the money?"

"All you have are three pice," says Sammi. "What can you buy for three pice?"

"I know what this clever fellow is up to," says Mahmood. "When we've spent all our money, he will buy sweets and tease us.

After the sweet-vendors there are a few hardware stores and shops of real and artificial jewellery. There is nothing there to attract the boys' attention, so they go ahead— all of them, except Hamid, who stops to see a pile of tongs. It occurs to him that his granny does not have a pair of tongs. Each time she bakes chapattis, the iron plate burns her hands. If he were to buy her a pair of tongs she would be very pleased. She would never burn her fingers again; it would be a useful thing to have in the house. What use are toys? They are a waste of money. You can have some fun with them but only for a very short time. Then you forget all about them.

Hamid's friends have gone ahead. They are at a stall drinking sherbet. How selfish they are! They bought so many sweets but did not give him one.

No sooner my granny sees my pair of tongs, she will run up to take it from me and say, 'My child has brought me a pair of tongs,' and shower me with a thousand blessings. She will show it off to the neighbours' women-folk. Soon the whole village will be saying, 'Hamid has brought his granny a pair of tongs, how nice he is!' No one will bless the other boys for the toys they have got for themselves. One day my father will return, and my mother too. Then I will ask these chaps, 'Do you want any toys? How many?' I will give each one a basket full of toys and teach them how to treat friends.

Hamid asks the shopkeeper, "How much for this pair of tongs?"

The shopkeeper looks at him and seeing no older person with him replies, "It's not for you."

"Is it for sale or not?"

"Why should it not be for sale? Why else should I have bothered to bring it here?"

"Why then don't you tell me how much it is!"

"It will cost you six pice."

Hamid's heart sinks. "Let me have the correct price."

"All right, it will be five pice, bottom price. Take it or leave it."

Hamid steels his heart and says, "Will you give it to me for three?" He then proceeds to walk away lest the shopkeeper screams at him. But the shopkeeper does not scream. On the contrary, he calls Hamid back and gives him the pair of tongs. Hamid carries it on his shoulder as if it were a gun and struts up proudly to show it to his friends.

Mohsin laughs and says, "Are you crazy? What will you do with the tongs?" Hamid flings the tongs on the ground and replies, "Try and throw your water-carrier on the ground. Every bone in his body will break."

Mahmood says, "Are these tongs some kind of toy?"

"Why not?" retorts Hamid. "Place them across your shoulders and it is a gun; they can make the same clanging as a pair of cymbals. One smack and they will reduce all your toys to dust. My tongs are like a brave tiger." Sammi who had bought a small tambourine asks, "Will you exchange them for my tambourine? It is worth eight pice."

Hamid pretends not to look at the tambourine. "My tongs, if they wanted, could tear out the skin of your tambourine. All it has is a leather skin and all it can say is dhub, dhub. A drop of water could silence it forever.

My brave pair of tongs can weather water and storms, without budging an inch."

The pair of tongs wins over everyone to its side. But now no one has any money left and the fairground has been left far behind. It is well past 9 a.m. and the sun is getting hotter by the minute. Everyone is in a hurry to get home. Even if they talked their fathers into it, they could not get the tongs.

The boys divide into two factions. Mohsin, Mahmood, Sammi and Noorey on the one side, and Hamid by himself on the other. They are engaged in hot argument.

"Your tongs' face will burn in the fire every day," taunts Mohsin. He is sure that this will leave Hamid speechless. That is not so. Pat comes Hamid with the retort, "Mister, it is only the brave who can jump into a fire. Your miserable lawyers, policemen, and water-carriers will run like frightened women into their homes. Only such a champion as this tong can perform this feat of leaping into the fire."

Our three heroes are utterly squashed— almost as if a champion kite had been brought down from the heavens to the earth by a cheap, miserable paper imitation. Thus Hamid wins the field. His tongs are the champion. Neither Mohsin nor Mahmood, neither Noorey nor Sammi— nor anyone else can dispute the fact.

The others have spent between twelve to sixteen pice each and bought nothing worthwhile. Hamid's three-pice worth has carried the day. And no one can deny that toys are unreliable things: they break, while Hamid's tongs will remain as they are for years.

The boys begin to make terms of peace. Mohsin says, "Give me your tongs for a while, you can have my water-carrier for the same time."

Both Mahmood and Noorey similarly offer their toys. Hamid has no hesitation in agreeing to these terms. The tongs pass from one hand to another; and the toys are in turn handed to Hamid. How lovely they are!

Mohsin says, "No one will bless us for these toys."

Mahmood adds, "You talk of blessings! We may get a thrashing instead. My Amma is bound to say, 'Are these earthen toys all that you could find at the fair?"'

Hamid knew that no mother will be as pleased with the toys as his granny will be when she sees the tongs. All he had was three pice and he has no reason to regret the way he has spent them. And now, his tongs were the king of toys as well.

By eleven, the village was again agog with excitement. All those who had gone to the fair were back at home. Mohsin's little sister snatched the water-carrier out of his hands and began to dance with joy. Mister Water-carrier slipped out of her hand, fell on the ground and went to paradise. The brother and sister began to fight; both had lots to cry about. Their mother lost her temper because of the racket they were making and gave each two resounding slaps.

Noorey's lawyer met an end befitting his grand status. Two nails were driven into the wall, a plank put on them and a carpet of paper spread on the plank. The honourable counsel was seated like a king on his throne. Noorey began to wave a fan , made of bamboo leaf, over him. He knew that in the law courts there were khus curtains and electric fans. We do not know whether it was the breeze or the fan or something else that brought the honourable counsel down from his high pedestal to the depths of hell and reduced his gown to mingle with the dust, of which it was made.

Mahmood's policeman remained. He was immediately put on duty to guard the village. But this police constable was no ordinary mortal who could walk on his own two feet. He had to be provided a palanquin. This was a basket lined with tatters of discarded clothes of red colour for the policeman to recline in comfort. Mahmood picked up the basket and started on his rounds. His two younger brothers followed him lisping, "Shopkeepers, keep awake!" But night has to be dark; Mahmood stumbled, the basket slipped out of his hand. Mr. Constable with his gun crashed on the ground.

Now let's hear what happened to our friend Hamid. As soon as she heard his voice, Granny Ameena ran out of the house, picked him up and kissed him. Suddenly she noticed the tongs in his hand. "Where did you find these tongs?"

"I bought them."

"How much did you pay for them?"

"Three pice."

Granny Ameena beat her breast. "You are a stupid child! It is almost noon and you haven't had anything to eat or drink. And what do you buy— tongs! Couldn't you find anything better in the fair than this pair of iron tongs?"

Hamid replied in injured tones, "You burn your fingers on the iron plate. That is why I bought them."

The old woman's temper suddenly changed to love—not the kind which wastes away in spoken words. This love was mute, solid and seeped with tenderness. What a selfless child! What concern for others! What a big heart! How he must have suffered seeing other boys buying toys and gobbling sweets! How was he able to suppress his own feelings! Even at the fair he thought of his old grandmother. Granny Ameena's heart was too full for words.

Hamid the child became Hamid the old man, and old Granny Ameena became Ameena the little girl. Big tears fell from her eyes. She spread her apron and beseeched Allah's blessings for her grandchild.

BADE BHAI SAHAB

ELDER BROTHER

My elder brother was five years older than I was, but only three grades ahead. He'd begun his studies at the same age I had, but he didn't like the idea of moving hastily in an important matter like education. He wanted to lay a firm foundation for that great edifice, so he took two years to do one year's work; sometimes he even took three. If the foundations weren't well-made, how could the edifice endure?

I was nine, he was fourteen. He had full right by seniority to supervise and instruct me. And I was expected to accept every order of his as law.

By nature he was very studious. He was always sitting with a book open. And perhaps to rest his brain, he would sometimes draw pictures of birds, dogs and cats in the margin of his notebook. Occasionally he would write a name, word or a sentence ten or twenty times. He might copy a couplet out several times in beautiful letters or create new words which made no rhyme or reason.

I wasn't really very keen about studying. To pick up a book and sit with it for an hour was a tremendous effort. As soon as I found a chance I'd leave the hostel and go to the field and play marbles or fly paper kites or sometimes just meet a friend, what could be more fun? But as soon as I came back into the room and saw my brother's scowling face, I was petrified. His first question would be, 'Where were you?' Always this question, always asked in the same tone and the only answer I had was silence. I don't know why I couldn't manage to say that I'd just been outside playing.

'If you study English this way you'll be studying your whole life and you won't get one word right! Studying English is no laughing matter that anyone who wants to can learn. You've got to wear out your eyes morning and night and use every ounce of energy, then maybe you'll get to know the subject. And even then, it's just to say you have a smattering of it. Even great scholars can't write proper English, let alone be able to speak it. I ask you, how much of a blockhead are you that you can't learn a lesson by looking at me? You've seen with your own eyes how much I grind. No matter how many shows and carnivals there may be, have you ever seen me going to watch them? Every day there are cricket and hockey matches, but I don't go near them. I keep on studying all the time, and even so it takes me two years or even three for one grade. How do you expect to pass when you waste your time playing like this? Why waste our dad's hard-earned money?'

Hearing a dressing-down like this, I'd start to cry. My brother was an expert in the art of giving advice. He'd say such sarcastic words, overwhelm me with such good counsel that my spirits would collapse, my courage disappear. I'd think, 'Why don't I run away from school and go back home!? Why should I spoil my life fiddling with work that's beyond my capacity? But after an hour or two the cloud of despair would clear away and I'd resolve to study with all my might. I'd draw up a schedule on the spot. How could I start work without first making an outline, working out a plan! Get up at the crack of dawn, wash hands and face at six, eat a snack, sit down and study. From six to eight, English; eight to nine, Arithmetic; nine to nine-thirty, History; then meal-time and then off to school. A half hour's rest at 3.30 when I got back from school, Geography from four to five, Grammar from five to six, then a half hour's break in front of the hostel, six-thirty to seven, English composition; then supper. Translation from eight to nine, Hindi from nine to ten, from ten to eleven, Miscellaneous, and then to bed.

But it's one thing to draw up a schedule, another to follow it. It began to be neglected from the very first day. The inviting green expanse of the playground, the balmy winds, the commotion on the football field, the speed and flurries of volleyball would all draw me mysteriously and irresistibly. As soon as I was there, I forgot everything: the life-destroying schedule, the books that strained your eyes- I couldn't remember them at all. And then my big brother would have an occasion for sermons and scolding. I would stay well out of his way, try to keep out of his sight, come into the room on tiptoe so he wouldn't know. But if he spotted me, I'd just about die.

The yearly exams came round: my brother failed, I passed and even stood first in my class. Only two year's difference was left between him and me now. I could be a little proud of myself now and indeed my ego swell. My brother's sway over me was over. I began to freely take part in the games, my spirits ran high. One day, when I'd spent the whole morning playing stick-ball and came back exactly at meal-time, he said with all the air of pulling out a sword to rush at me, "I see you've passed this year and you're first in your class, and you've got stuck up about it. But my dear brother, even great men live to regret their pride, then who are you compared to them? You must have read about what happened to Ravan. Just to pass an exam isn't anything, the real thing is to develop your mind. Understand the significance of what you read. Ravan was master of the earth. Such kings are called 'Rulers of the World'. All the kings of the earth paid taxes to him. Great divinities were his slaves, even the gods of fire and water. But what happened to him in the end? Pride completely finished him off, destroying even his name. There wasn't anybody left to perform all his funeral rites properly. A man can commit any sin he wants but he'd better not be proud. When he turns proud he loses both this world and the next. You've just been promoted one grade and your head's turned by it.

'Don't assume that because I failed I'm stupid and you're smart. When you reach my class you'll sweat right through your teeth when you have to bite into algebra and geometry and study English, and History. It's not easy to memorize these king's names. There were eight Henrys! Do you think it's easy to remember all the things that happened in each Henry's time? If you write Henry the Eighth instead of Henry the Seventh, you get a zero. There were dozens of James, dozens of Williams and scores of Charles! You get dizzy with them, your mind's in a whirl. Those poor fellows didn't have names enough to go around. After every name they have to put second, third, fourth and fifth. If anybody'd asked me, I could have reeled off thousands of names.

'As for geometry, well God help you! If you write *a c b* instead of *a b c* your whole answer is marked wrong. But you've got to pass so you've got to memorize all.

'They say, 'Write an essay on punctuality no less than four pages long.' Who doesn't know that punctuality's a very good thing! A man's life is organized according to it, others love him for it and his business prospers from it. How can you write four pages on something so trifling! Do I need four pages for what I can describe in one sentence? It's not economizing time, it's wasting it. We want a man to say what he has to say quickly and then get moving. It's a contradiction for them to ask us to write concisely. Write a concise essay on punctuality in no less than four pages. All right! If four pages is concise then maybe otherwise they'd ask us to write one or two hundred pages. Run fast and walk slow at the same time. Is that all mixed up. When you get into my class, you'll really take a beating, and then you'll find out what's what. Just because you got a first division this time, you're all puffed up, so pay attention to what I say.

'What if I failed, I'm still older than you. I have more experience of the world. Take what I say to heart or you'll be sorry.'

It was almost time for school, otherwise I don't know when this medley of sermons would have ended. I didn't have much appetite that day. If I got a scolding like this when I passed, had I failed, I would have had to pay with my life. My brother's terrible description of studying in the ninth grade really scared me. I'm surprised I didn't run away from school and go home. But even a scolding like this didn't change my distaste for books a bit. I didn't miss one chance to play. I studied, but much less. Well, just enough to complete the day's assignments and not be disgraced in class. The confidence, however, that I'd gained in myself disappeared and then I began to lead a life like a thief.

Then it was the yearly exams again and it so happened that once more I passed and my brother failed again. I hadn't done much work, but somehow I was in the first division. I was astonished myself. My brother had just about killed himself with work, memorizing every word in the course, studying till ten at night and starting again at four in the morning, and from six until 9.30 before going to school. He'd grown pale. But the poor fellow failed again and I felt sorry for him. When he heard the results he broke down and cried and so did I. My pleasure in passing was cut by half. There was only one grade left between my brother and me. The evil thought crossed my mind that if he failed just once more I'd be at the same level as him and then what grounds would he have for lecturing me! But I violently rejected this unworthy idea. After all, he'd scolded me only with the intention of helping me. I thought that maybe it was only as a result of his advice that I'd passed so easily and with such good marks.

Now my brother had become much gentler toward me. Several times when he found occasion to scold me, he did it without losing his temper. Perhaps he himself was beginning to understand that he no longer had the right to tell me off, or at least not so much as before. My independence grew. I began to take unfair advantage of his toleration. I half started to imagine that I'd pass next time whether I studied or not, my luck was high. As a result, the little I used to study because of my brother before, even that ceased. I found a new pleasure in flying kites and spent all my time at the sport. Still, I minded my manners with my brother and concealed my kite-flying from him. In preparation for the kite tournament, I was secretly busy solving such problems as how best to secure the string and how to apply the paste mixed with ground glass on it to cut the other fellows' kites off their strings. I didn't want to let my brother suspect that my respect for him had in any way diminished.

One day, far from the hostel, I was running along like mad trying to grab hold of a kite. A whole army of boys came racing out to welcome it with long, thick bamboo rods. Nobody was aware who was in front or at the back of him. Suddenly, I collided with my brother who was probably coming back from the market. He grabbed my hand and said angrily, 'Aren't you ashamed to be running with these ragamuffins after a one-paisa kite? Have you forgotten that you're not in a low grade anymore? You’re in the eighth now, just one behind me. A man's got to have some regard for his position after all.

'I'm sorry to see you have so little sense. You're smart, there's no doubt of that, but what use is it if it destroys your self-respect? You must have assumed, ‘I'm just one grade behind my brother so now he doesn't have any right to say anything to me,’ but you're mistaken. I'm five years older than you and even if you come into my grade today, that difference of five years between us cannot be erased by God himself. I'm five years older than you and always will be. The experience I have of life and the world, you can never catch up with even if you get an M.A. or a D.Litt. or even a Ph.D. Understanding doesn't come from reading books. Our mother never passed any grade and Dad probably never went beyond the fifth, but even if we studied the wisdom of the whole world, mother and father would always have the right to correct us. Not just because they're our parents, but because they'll always have more experience of the world. Maybe they don't know what kind of government they've got in America or how many constellations there are in the sky, but there are a thousand things they know more about than you or me. God forbid, but if I should fall sick today, you'd be at your wit's end. You wouldn't be able to think of anything except sending a telegram to Dad. But in your place, he wouldn't send anybody a telegram or get upset or be all flustered. First of all, he'd diagnose the disease himself and try the remedy, then if it didn't work, he'd call some doctor. But you and I don't even know how to make our allowance last through the month. We spend what father sends us and then we're penniless again. For as much as you and I spend today, Dad's maintained himself honourably and in good reputation for the greater part of his life and brought up a family on just half of it. So brother, don't be so proud of having almost caught up with me and being independent now. I'll see that you don't go off the track. I know you don't like hearing all this.'

I was thoroughly shamed by this new approach of his. I had truly come to know my own insignificance and a new respect for my brother was born in my heart. With tears in my eyes, I said, 'No, no, what you say is completely true and you have the right to say it.' My brother embraced me and said, 'I don't forbid you to fly kites. I'd like to too. But what can I do? If I go off-the track myself, how will I watch out for you? That's my responsibility.' Just then, a kite that had been cut loose passed over us, by chance, with its string dangling down. A crowd of boys were chasing after it. My brother is very tall and leaping up. He caught hold of the string and ran at top speed toward the hostel. I ran close behind him, leaving all the other boys behind.

PANCH-PARMESHWAR

THE HOLY PANCHAYAT

Jumman Sheikh and Algu Chowdhry were very close friends. They were partners in cultivation. They trusted each other without reservation. When Jumman had gone on hajj - his sacred pilgrimage, he had left his house under Algu's care. And whenever Algu went out he left his house to Jumman to look after. They neither dined the same way, nor were they of the same religion. But there was between them a certain concurrence of views. And that indeed is the basis of true friendship.

Their friendship began when they were boys, and Jumman's worshipful father, Jumeraati, was their tutor. Algu had served his guru with great diligence, washing many plates and cups. Algu's father was old-fashioned in his views. He believed that serving the guru was more important than acquiring knowledge. He would say that one acquired knowledge, not by reading books but through the guru's blessings. Therefore, if Jumeraati Shaikh's blessings him did not yield results, he would then rest content with the thought that he had tried his best but he did not succeed because it was not so destined that Algu should acquire knowledge.

However, Jumeraati Shaikh himself did not subscribe to this view. He had greater faith in his rod. And because of that rod, Jumman was greatly admired in the villages around here. Not even the court clerk could raise any objection to the documents prepared by Jumman. The postman, the constable and the tehsil peon – all looked up to him. As a result, while Algu was respected for his money, Jumman Shaikh was esteemed for his invaluable knowledge.

...

Jumman Shaikh had an old aunt who had some property. She had no other near relations besides Jumman. He had coaxed her into transferring this property in his name by making tall promises. Until the transfer deed had been registered, the aunt was pampered and indulged. She was treated to many tasty dishes. It was raining puddings and pulaos; but this hospitality came to a stamping halt as soon as the transfer deed was stamped. Jumman's wife, Kariman, began to dish out, along with chapatis, hot and bitter curries of words. Jumman Shikh too became hard-hearted. Now the poor aunt had to swallow bitter words every day:

God knows how long would this old woman live! She thinks she has bought us by just transferring a few bighas of barren land. And chapatis don't go down her throat if her dal is not fried in ghee! We would have bought a whole village with the amount of money she has already swallowed!

Khala listened to all this for a few days, and when she could stand it no longer she complained to Jumman. Jumman didn't think it right to interfere in what was the domain of the mistress of the house. And this state of affairs dragged on for some more time. At last, the aunt said to Jumman, 'Son, I can't carry on like this. You pay me a sum regularly. I shall set up my own kitchen.'

Jumman retorted rudely, 'Do you think we grow money here?'

Khala asked politely, 'Do I not need a bare minimum to survive?'

Jumman replied sternly, 'We had never thought you had conquered death.'

Khala was offended. She threatened to call the Panchayat. Jumman laughed heartily like the hunter who laughs to himself as he watches the deer walking into his trap. He said, 'Why not? Call the Panchayat by all means. Let things be decided once for all. I don't like this daily bickering.'

Jumman had no doubt at all who would win at the panchayat. There was no one in the villages around who did not owe him a debt of gratitude; no one who would dare to antagonize him. God's angels won't come down to hold the Panchayat.

...

After this, for many days, leaning on her stick, the old woman hopped from village to village. Her back was bent like a bow. Each step was painful. But the issue had to be settled.

There was hardly a soul to whom she did not narrate her tale of woe. A few dismissed her story with just lip sympathy. Some decried the world in general. 'One may have one's foot in the grave, yet there is no end to greed! What does a person need? Eat your bread and remember Allah. Why bother about land and tilling now?' There were some who got an opportunity to poke fun at her. Bent back, toothless mouth, matted hair – so much to laugh at! Just, kind and compassionate people who would listen to this unfortunate woman's sad story and console her were few indeed. Finally, she came to Algu Chowdhry's door. She threw down her stick and sat down to rest. Then she said, 'Son, you should also come to the Panchayat meeting.'

Algu said, 'Why call me? There will be many people from the villages around.'

The old woman said, 'I have cried my heart out to all. But now it's up to them to come.'

Algu said, 'I shall come, but I won't open my mouth.'

'Why, son?'

'My will. Jumman is my old friend. I can't go against him.'

'Son, won't you stand up for justice for fear of losing your friendship?'

Algu had no answer to this question, but these words were echoing in his mind.

...

One evening the Panchayat gathered under a tree. Shaikh Jumman had spread his sheets well in advance. He had made provision for paan, ilaichi, hookah and tobacco. He himself was sitting with Algu Chowdhry at some distance. He greeted with a discrete salaam everyone who had come to attend the panchayat meeting. Soon after sunset, when the flocks of chattering birds had settled in the tree, the meeting began. Every inch of the ground was occupied, but most of those who had come were onlookers. Of those the old woman had requested, only they who had a grudge against Jumman had come. A fire had been lighted in one corner. Boys were running all around, shouting, crying. It was a noisy scene. The village dogs too had descended upon the scene in large numbers, hoping there would be a big feast here.

The members of the Panchayat sat down and the old woman began her submission.

'Members of the Panchayat, it's three years now, since I transferred all my property in the name of my nephew Jumman. You know all this. Jumman had promised to feed and clothe me till my death. But I neither get enough to eat nor to wear. I have put up with it for a year. I can stand it no longer. I'm a helpless widow. I can't go to court. Where else should I come with my miserable tale except to you? I shall accept whatever you decide. If I'm at fault, punish me. If Jumman is wrong, admonish him. Why does he want to earn the curses of a helpless woman? Panchayat's word is the word of Allah. I shall obey the Panchayat's order without question.'

Ramdhan Misra, many of whose clients had been won over by Jumman, said, 'Jumman mian, choose your Panchayat. Decide just now. Afterwards you will have to accept its judgement.'

Jumman saw that most of those present here were hostile to him for one reason or another. He said, 'The word of the Panchayat is the word of Allah. Let khala choose whomsoever she wants. I have no objection.'

The old woman shouted. 'O man of Allah, why don't you name the members?'

Jumman retorted angrily, 'Don't force me to open my mouth. You have complained. Choose whomsoever you like.'

The aunt understood Jumman's taunt. She said, 'Son, fear Allah. What're you insinuating. Members of panchayat don't take sides. And if you can't trust any-one, let it go. I hope you trust Algu Chowdhry. Come on, I choose him as the Panchayat head.'

Jumman was delighted, but hiding his feelings he said, 'Let it be Algu. For me, Ramdhan Misra and Algu are the same.'

Algu didn't want to get involved in this. He said, 'Khala, you know that Jumman is my close friend.'

Khala said, 'Son, no one barters his imaan for friend-ship. Allah resides in the heart of a panch. Whatever the panch says is the word of Allah.'

Algu Chowdhry was designated the Sarpanch. Ramdhan Mishra and some others hostile to Jumman, cursed the old woman in their hearts.

Algu Chowdry said, 'Shaikh Jumman, you and I are old friends. We have helped each other on many occasions. But at this moment, we are not friends. You and khaala are equal in my eyes. You can put forward your case before the Panchayat.'

Jumman was sure that he would win the case. Algu was saying all this for a public show. Therefore he spoke in a very composed manner. 'O members of the Panchayat, three years ago, khaala jaan transferred her property in my name. I had agreed to provide her with food and clothing till her death. Allah is witness, I have never ill-treated her. I regard her as my mother and it is my duty to serve her. My wife and she don't always see eye to eye. What can I do in this? Khaala jaan is demanding a monthly allowance from me separately. All of you know the value of the property. It is not so profitable that I can provide a monthly allowance to her out of it. Moreover, there is no mention of a monthly expense in the agreement. That's all I have to say. It is now for the members of the Panchayat to give their judgement.'

Algu Chowdhry needed to go to the court regularly for some or other of his business. This had made him a completely legal minded person. He began to cross examine Jumman. Every word he said was like a hammer stroke on Jumman's chest. Ramdhan Mishra was enjoying it all. Jumman was taken aback at Algu's conduct. Just a few moments ago, he was talking to him like a friend, and now he seemed so changed and bent upon pulling him up by the roots. Was he trying to settle some old score? Will his long friendship be of no help?

While Jumman Shaikh was lost in this mental tussle, Algu announced the judgement.

'Shaikh Jumman, the Panchayat has considered this matter. To us, it looks fair and just that khaala jaan be given a monthly allowance. We are of the view that the property is valuable enough to provide khaala jaan a monthly allowance. This is our decision. And if this is not acceptable to you, then the agreement for transfer of property would stand annulled.'

Jumman was stunned to hear this decision. Your own friend slitting your throat! What else would you call it except the trickery of time? The very person on whom you had all the faith betrayed you when you needed him most. Such are the times when friendship is tested. So that is what friendship is in this day and age. It is such crooked and deceitful people who have brought so many calamities upon the country. The epidemics like cholera and plague were the punishment for such misdeeds.

On the other hand, Ramdhan Mishra and other members of the Panchayat were heartily praising Algu Chowdhry's sense of justice. They said, 'This is what a Panchayat is. He has separated the grain from the chaff. Friendship has its own place but to follow the dharma is the most important thing. The earth has stayed where it is because of such truthful people or it would have sunk underwater by now.'

This judgement shook the very foundation of Algu and Jumman's friendship. The old intimacy was gone. If such an old tree of friendship could not stand just one blast of truth, surely it had stood on sandy ground.

Now their relationship turned very formal, and limited to mere courtesies. They met but just as a sword meets a shield.

Algu's treachery troubled Jumman day and night. He was always looking for an opportunity to take revenge.

...

The chance for doing a good deed takes a long time to come, but not so in the case of a bad deed. And the opportunity to take revenge came to Jumman very soon. A year ago Algu Chowdhry had purchased a fine pair of oxen from Batesar. The oxen were of the Pachchain breed, handsome and with long horns. For months, people from the neighbouring villages came to cast their admiring glances at the pair. It was just a chance that one of the oxen died just a month after Jumman's panchayat. Jumman said to his friends, 'This is punishment for his treachery. One may rest content but God keeps watch on our good and bad deeds.' Algu on the other hand began to suspect that Jumman had poisoned the ox. His wife too threw the blame on Jumman. She said Jumman had done some mischief. One day, a war of words broke out between Algu's wife and Kariman. Words flowed in great streams from both the sides. All the similes and metaphors, sarcasms and hyperboles were exhausted. Jumman somehow pacified them. He rebuked his wife into silence and made her quit the battlefield. On the other side Algu did the same to silence his wife.

Now, a single ox was of no use. Algu tried to find a matching one, but without success. At last, he decided to sell it off. There was a trader named Samjhu Sahuji who drove a single-ox cart. He carried gur and ghee from the village to the market and returned with oil and salt, which he sold in the village. He thought of buying this ox. If he had this ox, he would be able to make three trips easily. With his old ox, it was difficult to make even one. He looked at the ox, yoked it to his cart for a trial, got the hair on its body examined to know whether it was a propitious animal to buy, bargained the price and finally bought it. He promised to pay the price within one month. Algu Chowdhry agreed, unmindful of any loss.

As soon as Samjhu Sahuji had the ox, he began to drive it hard. He made three to four trips every day, without caring to feed the animal properly. All he cared was to drive him. When he took him to the market he fed him with some dry fodder. And before he could breathe easy, he was yoked again. At Algu Chowdhry's home, the ox had had a placid existence. He was yoked to a chariot-like cart once in a while and then he would go racing for miles without care. At Algu's house, his daily diet consisted of clean water, ground arhar dal, fodder mixed with oil cake, and on occasions, he had the pleasure of tasting ghee too. From morning till evening an attendant looked after him, brushed his hair, cleaned and patted his body. That life of peace and enjoyment, and this twenty-four hour drudgery! He became emaciated in just a month. The moment he saw the yoke, his mouth dried up. Moving even a step had become difficult. Bones had become visible, but he was self-respecting and didn't like to be beaten or whipped.

One day, while on his fourth trip, Samjhu Sahuji put a double load on him. Exhausted after the day's work, the ox was unable to lift his feet, but Sahuji kept on whipping him. He ran with all his strength, and after a short distance slowed down to regain his breath. But Sahuji, in a hurry to reach home, kept on lashing at him with his whip. He tried to pick up pace once again, but his strength failed. He collapsed and did not rise again.

Sahuji whipped him mercilessly, pulled his legs, pushed a stick into his nostrils, but how could a dead animal rise on his feet? When Sahuji suspected the worst, he cast an intent look at the ox, then unyoked him, wondering how to drive the cart home. He shouted but the country pathways, like the eyes of children, closed at sunset. He could not find any help. There was no village close by. In anger he delivered a few more lashes to the dead animal, shouting that he should have died after reaching home. Who would pull the cart now? Sahuji was burning with anger. He had sold many sacks of gur and many tins of ghee and was carrying a few hundred rupees with him too. In addition, there were a few sacks of salt and tins of oil on the cart. He just couldn't leave them here. Helpless, he decided to spend the night in the cart. He tried to keep awake till midnight. He thought he had kept awake throughout, but when he opened his eyes at the break of day and touched his waist he found the pouch containing the money missing. A few tins of oil were also missing. In anguish the poor man beat his head and fell flat on the ground. He reached home wailing and weeping. When Sahuji's wife heard the story, first she cried and then started cursing Algu Chowdhry for having sold them an unpropitious ox that had caused the loss of their life-long earning.

Many months passed. Whenever Algu went to their house to ask for the price of the ox both husband and wife fell upon him like dogs and started abusing him. 'Look, we have lost our life's earnings and you are asking for the price of the ox. You had given us a near dead ox and now you want its price. You have deceived us. You hoodwinked us to buy a ruinous animal. Do you think we are fools? We can't be fooled like children. If you don't accept this, take our ox and use it for two months. What else do you want?'

Chowdhry had plenty of ill-wishers. On this occasion, they came together to support Sahuji. It was not easy for Algu to give up his claim of one hundred fifty rupees. He lost his cool one day. Sahuji went home to look for a lathi, and his wife took his place to confront Algu. Arguments led to fighting. Sahuji's wife ran home and shut the doors. The villagers gathered there on hearing the hullabaloo. They tried to pacify both the parties. But this didn't work. They asked for a Panchayat to be called to settle the issue. Sahuji agreed. Algu agreed too.

...

Preparations for the Panchayat began. Both the parties began to look for their supporters. On the third day, the Panchayat assembled under the same tree, at the same evening time.

The Panchayat began its meeting. Ramdhan Mishra said, 'Why waste time? Let us elect the five members. Come Chowdhry, whom do you elect?'

Algu said in a humble voice, 'Let Samjhu Sahu choose.'

Samjhu stood up and said sharply, 'I choose Jumman Shaikh.'

The moment Algu heard Jumman's name, his heart began to beat fast as if some had slapped him. Ramdhan was Algu's friend. He could sense the problem. He said, 'Chowdhry, do you have any objection?'

Chowdhry said in a thin voice, 'No, why should I object?'

The awareness of a responsibility often alters our narrow outlook. When we lose our way this awareness becomes our guide.

Jumman Shaikh also became conscious of such a responsibility, the moment he assumed the high office of the sarpanch. He realized that at this moment he was seated on the highest throne of justice and righteousness.

Whatever he uttered now would be the word of God, and any prejudice of his mind must not contaminate that voice. He must not deviate even a tiny bit from truth.

The Panchayat began to interrogate both the parties. Both the parties pleaded their cases. There was a difference of opinion among the members of the Panchayat. All were agreed that Samjhu Sahu must pay the price of the ox, but two members were of the view that he should be given some relief for the loss of the ox. Against this, two members wanted Samjhu to be punished further, in addition to the appropriate payment, so that no one in future would dare to behave with such barbarity towards an animal. In the end Jumman announced the judgement.

'Algu Chowhdry and Samjhu Sahu, the Panchayat has carefully deliberated on your dispute. It is proper that Samjhu should pay the price of the ox. The ox was not suffering from any disease when he bought it. If the price had been paid then, Samjhu would not have been able to raise this question. The ox died because he was forced to work too hard and was not properly fed.'

Ramdhan said, 'Samjhu is responsible for killing the ox and he should be punished for this.'

Jumman said, 'That is another issue. We have nothing to do with it.'

Jhagdu Sahu said, 'Samjhu Sahu should be given some relief.'

Jumman said, 'This is up to Algu Chowdhry. If he agrees, it will be an act of goodness.'

Algu Chowdhry was overjoyed. He stood up and shouted, 'Victory to Panch-parmeshwar!'

This was echoed from all sides, 'Victory to Panch-parmeshwar.'

Everyone admired Jumman's judgement. 'This is justice. This is not the work of man. God himself resides in the Panch-parmeshwar. It is His doing. Who can prove the wrong as right before the Panchayat!'

At the end, Jumman came to Algu and embraced him, saying, 'Ever since you had given the judgement against me, I had become your sworn enemy. But today, I have realized that while sitting on that seat of justice, you are no one's friend or foe. You cannot think of anything except justice. Today, I am convinced that God himself speaks through the voice of the Panchayat.'

• • •

Algu began to cry. His tears washed off the bitterness that had rankled in their hearts. The withered plant of friendship had become green again.

• • •

PAREEKSHA

THE TEST

When Sardar Sujan Singh, Diwan of the State of Devgarh, reached the dusk of his life, he remembered God. He went to the Maharaja and said, 'O, friend of the oppressed, this slave has served you for forty long years. I now seek your permission to serve God for some time. I'm far advanced in years and have no energy left to handle the administration of the state. I don't want to sully my name by some unintended mistake and ruin my reputation earned through a life-long service.'

Raja Sahib had great respect for his very experienced and statesman-like Diwan. He tried to persuade him to continue, but when Diwan Sahib did not budge, he acceded to his request but on the condition that he himself will have to select the new Diwan.

The next day, the important newspapers of the country carried this advertisement for the appointment to the office of Diwan for the state: Anyone who considers himself suitable for appointment to this office should present himself before the present Diwan, Sardar Sujan Singh. He need not be a graduate, but should be strongly built. Those suffering from weak stomachs need not take the trouble to come. All the aspirants would be treated as guests and kept under observation for their behaviour and character. More than education, commitment to duty would be rewarded. One who came up to these expectations would be appointed to this high office.

...

The advertisement created a furore in the country. Such an exalted office, and no qualifications! It all seemed a matter of chance. Hundreds set out to try their luck and Devgarh became the destination for all varieties of people. From every train a whole bunch of visitors deboarded. Some came from Madras, others from Punjab. Some showing off their simplicity, others displaying the latest fashions. Pandits and maulvis also saw an opportunity to test their fortunes. Poor fellows had always rued the lack of degrees, but here there was no need for them. Colourful cloaks and chogas, and all varieties of fancy wear and head-dresses were now on display in Devgarh. However, the largest number were still of degree holders, for even if it was not required, a degree did act as a fig leaf.

Sardar Sujan Singh had made very good arrangements to accommodate and entertain the guests. Lodged in their rooms, the candidates counted each day like a Muslim does during Ramazan. Every visitor tried to showcase his life in the best manner possible. Mr. A, who used to get up at nine, was seen strolling in the park before sunrise. Mr. B, who was addicted to the hookah, now smoked cigars behind closed doors. Some others, who at home treated their servants like slaves, talked to the servants here with unusual courtesy and politeness. Mr. K, who was an atheist, had become so religious that even the temple priests might have felt threatened with dismissal. Yet another, Mr. L, who hated books, was lost in browsing through great big books these days. Everyone seemed to be a model of gentleness and good conduct. Sharma ji spent his time reciting mantras from the Vedas and the maulvi sahib had nothing else to do except reciting the Quran. Each one thought it was just a one-month botheration, and once he had succeeded, who would care.

But that discerning old jeweller was inconspicuously observing everyone, trying to spot the swan among the cranes.

...

One day, a fashionable group proposed playing a hockey match. This proposal was made by some seasoned players of the game. After all, this too was an art, why not show it off? Who knew whether this might help. The decision was taken, the teams formed and the match began. The ball began to be pushed and thrashed like some office equipment.

This game was altogether new for Devgarh. The literate and the respectable people played thoughtful games like chess and cards. Games involving running and jumping were believed to be children's games.

The match turned out to be a spirited contest. When the attacking side rushed forward with the ball, they looked like a wave surging forward, but the defending side stood like a wall of steel to check its advance.

It went on till the evening. The players were drenched in sweat, their faces red with heat. They were gasping for breath, and the match ended in a draw.

It was dark now. There was a wide drain close to the playground. There was no bridge over the drain and the wayfarers had to wade through it to get to the other side. The play had just ended and the players were resting to regain their breath. Just then, a farmer came to the drain with a cart-full of grain. Partly because the track was muddy and partly because the climb was steep, he was unable to drive the cart up through the drain. He yelled at the bullocks; he tried to push the wheels up with his own hands, but the cart was quite overloaded and the bullocks just not strong enough. The poor fellow looked around, but found no help. He could not leave the cart unattended and go somewhere else to seek help. He was in great trouble. At that very moment, the players happened to pass by carrying their sticks. The farmer looked at them with pleading eyes, but didn't have the courage to ask for help. The players also looked at him, but with an unresponsive gaze, with eyes that reflected no sympathy and drunk with pride, showing no sign of generosity or compassion.

Among the players however, there was one person who had both sympathy and courage. He had hurt his foot during the match and was slowly limping along. Suddenly, his eyes fell on the cart and he stopped. The moment he looked at the farmer, he understood the situation. He kept his stick on one side, removed his coat and said to the farmer, 'Should I help you push your cart up?'

The farmer saw in front of him a tall well-built man. 'Hazoor, I dare not ask you.' The young man said, 'It seems you have been stranded here for a long time. Go and sit on the cart and direct the bullocks while I push the wheels up.'

The farmer went and sat in the cart. The young man pushed the cart up. The whole place was muddy and he was driven up to his knees into the mud. Yet, he didn't give up. He pushed the cart again. The farmer shouted at his bullocks. The bullocks got support, regained their courage and with a last effort, they pulled the cart out of the drain.

The farmer stood before the youth with folded hands and said, 'Maharaj, you have done a great favour to me. Otherwise, I would have had to spend the whole night here.'

The young man said jokingly, 'Now, would you give me some reward?'

The farmer said, 'God willing, you will be the Diwan.'

The young man looked at the farmer. He wondered whether the farmer was Sujan Singh himself. He had the same voice, the same face. The farmer looked at the youth with a quick eye too. Perhaps, he sensed what the young man was thinking. He smiled and said, 'One finds pearls only by diving into deep waters.'

...

The period of one month was over. The day of reckoning arrived. All the candidates were anxious to know what destiny had in store for them. The wait seemed like crossing a mountain. Hope and dejection crossed their faces like shadows. No one knew who was to be the lucky one, the goddess Lakshmi's favourite.

In the evening, the Raja sahib held his court. The city's rich and famous, the officers of the state, the courtiers, and the candidates for the office of the Diwan – all were assembled in the court, dressed in their best. The candidates' hearts were beating fast.

Sujan Singh got up and said, 'Aspirants for the position of the Diwan, forgive me for any trouble that I might have given you. For this office, I needed a person who was full of compassion and generosity, someone who had great determination to face any difficulty. Fortunately, the state has discovered such a person. People who possess such qualities are few in this world and are already holding high offices, so we cannot approach them. I congratulate the state to have Pandit Jankinath as the new Diwan.

The officers and the wealthy of the state looked at Jankinath with appreciation, the candidates with envy.

Sardar Sahib spoke again, 'I believe you will not hesitate to accept that a person who, in spite of being injured, should help a poor farmer to drag his cart out of mud must be compassionate and strong-willed. Such a person would never oppress the poor. His determination will keep his heart steady. He may be deceived, but would not budge from the path of duty.'

SUBHAAGI

Whatever others might say, Tulsi Mehto loved his daughter, Subhagi, no less than he loved his son, Ramu. Although grown up, Ramu remained a simpleton, but Subhagi was so clever with the household work and such an accomplished farmhand that her mother, Lakshmi, feared that the Gods might cast a covetous eyes on her, for even God loved good children. To prevent people from praising Subhagi too much, she would deliberately find fault with her. She did not fear that Subhagi would be spoiled by praise, but she feared the evil eye. The same Subhagi become a widow at eleven.

The whole house fell into disarray. Lakshmi fell down unconscious. Tulsi beat his head. Watching them, Subhagi also cried. She repeatedly said to her mother, 'Stop crying, I won't desert you.' Her mother was broken-hearted, listening to Subhagi's naïve talk. She wondered 'O God, you play strange games, inflicting pain on others like this. Why play games that amuse you, but hurt others? People call you compassionate. And this is your compassion!'

...

As Subhagi grew into adulthood, people started urging Tulsi Mehto to marry her off again. It wasn't proper to let a young girl move around like that. When their community did not object to remarriage, why should he hesitate?

Tulsi replied, 'I'm ready, but Subhagi isn't willing at all.'

Harihar said to her, 'Beti, we're saying all this for your own good. Your parents are old. How long would they live? You can't go on like this forever.'

Subhagi replied, with her head bowed down, 'Chacha, I understand what you say. But my heart is not in it. I don't think of my own life. I can face anything. Ask me anything else and I shall do it willingly, but not this. If you ever find me transgressing the society's bounds, cut my head off. I give you my word. But who am I to make such claims? It is for God to protect my honour.'

Ramu spoke out rudely, 'If you think I shall toil to feed you for your entire life, you're mistaken. I'm under no obligation to feed you for a lifetime.' His wife held the same sentiments towards Subhagi.

Subhagi replied in a dignified manner, 'Bhabi, I have never sought your protection, and God willing, I shall never do so in future. Take care of yourself and don't worry about me.'

When Ramu's wife realized that Subhagi won't take a husband, she started nagging her continuously, finding fault with her. She enjoyed hurting her. Subhagi would get up early in the morning and get busy pounding-grinding, cooking-washing, making dung cakes, and then she would go and work in the field. She would come back in the afternoon and cook for everyone and feed them. At night, she would oil her mother's head and massage her body. She tried her utmost not to make her parents work, but she didn't spare her brother. He was young and if he did not work, how would the household run?

Ramu did not like that Subhagi should let their parents sit idle and force him to work. One day he burst out and said to Subhagi, 'If you love them so much, go and start living with them and away from us. Only then will you realize whether serving someone is a pleasure or pain. To earn praise by living on others' toil is easy. He alone is brave who lives on his own labour.'

Subhagi didn't answer back, fearing that things would come to a breaking point, but their parents were listening. Mehto couldn't control himself. He said, 'Ramu, why are you quarrelling with that poor girl?'

Ramu turned to him and said, 'Why're you jumping in? I'm talking to her.'

Tulsi retorted, 'So long as I am alive, you can't speak to her like this. You have made her life hell.'

Ramu said, 'If you love your daughter so much, tie her round your neck. I can't stand her any more.'

Tulsi said, 'All right, if this is what you want, so be it. Tomorrow, I shall call the village elders and ask for a division. I'm willing to lose you, but not Subhagi.'

At night, when Tulsi lay down to sleep, he remembered something. When Ramu was born, he had borrowed money to celebrate, but when Subhagi was born, he had not spent even a penny, even though he was not short of money. He had regarded the son as a diamond and the daughter as a punishment for their sins in the previous life. And now, the diamond had proved too hard and the punishment so favourable!

...

The next day, Mehto called the villagers in and said, 'Members of the panchayat, Ramu and I cannot live together anymore. I want you to make a just division and allocate me whatever is my share. I can't stand the daily bickering anymore.'

The village headman, Babu Sajan Singh, was a sensible person. He spoke to Ramu, 'Tell me, do you want to break with your father? Aren't you ashamed to break with your parents just because your wife wants it? O, Ram!'

Ramu replied brazenly, 'When you can't live together, it's better to part.'

'What's your problem in living together?'

'There're many.'

'Tell me one.'

'In one word, I can't live with them. That's all I know.'

Saying this, Ramu walked away.

Tulsi said, 'Look at his temper. You may allocate him three-fourths of what we have, but I can't live with this wretched fellow. God has been unkind to my daughter; otherwise I won't have cared about the land. I could have managed to live by my labour anywhere. Such a son shouldn't be born even to my worst enemy. A caring daughter is far better than such a son.'

Suddenly Subhagi arrived at the scene. She said, 'Dada, I'm the root cause of this division. Why don't you separate me? I'll live by my labour and help you as far as I can, but I shall live alone. I can't stand this division of the family. I can't live with this blot on my name.'

Tulsi said, 'Daughter, we won't let you go, even if we lose our life. I don't ever want to see Ramu's face again. Living with him is out of the question.'

Ramu's wife retorted, 'If you don't want to see our faces, we too aren't dying to serve you.'

Mehto, gnashing his teeth, rose to thrash his daughter-in-law, but people stopped him.

...

After the division, Lakshmi and Mehto became a retired couple. Before this, in spite Subhagi's protests, they would keep doing something or the other, but now they were fully at leisure. Before this, they used to crave for ghee and milk. Now, Subhagi purchased a buffalo for them from the money that she had saved. Mehto opposed the purchase, saying that she was overburdening herself with this additional work, but Subhagi put him off saying that she loved milk. Lakshmi said, laughing, 'Beti, don't tell lies. You don't even touch milk and force us to drink all of it.'

In the village, everyone praised Subhagi. 'She is not a woman but a goddess,' they said. 'She works like two men, and more than that, she takes care of her parents.'

However, Mehto was not destined to enjoy this state of well-being for long. He had been down with fever for more than a week. He didn't allow even a thin layer of clothing on his body. Lakshmi sat by him, crying. Subhagi was there too, holding a vessel of water. A moment ago, he had asked for water, but just as she brought it, Mehto's heart sunk and his body went cold. Realizing this grave situation, Subhagi ran to Ramu's house and said, 'Bhaiyya, dada's condition is very serious. He has been down with fever for a week.'

Ramu, who was lying on his cot, said, 'Am I a doctor that I should go and see him? So long as he was hale and hearty, you were hanging round his neck like a garland, and now when he is dying, you have come to me.'

Just then, Ramu's wife came out and asked, 'What's wrong with dada, didi?'

Even before Subhagi could speak, Ramu spoke out, 'Oh nothing. He's not dying.'

Subhagi said nothing. She went straight to Sajan Singh. After she was gone, Ramu said to his wife laughing, 'This is what you call female trickery.'

'What trickery? Why don't to go?'

'I won't go. Let them manage on their own. I won't go even if he dies.'

His wife said laughing, 'If he dies, you will have to light his pyre. You won't be able to run away then.'

'Never. His beloved Subhagi would have to do everything.'

• • •

'Why would she do it when you're there?'

'Because he broke with me, preferring her over me.'

'No, this is not right. Let's go and see him. After all, he's your father. You won't be able to show your face in the village.'

'Keep quiet. Don't preach to me.'

On the other hand, the moment Babu sahib learnt about Mehto's condition, he came to see him at once. Mehto's condition had worsened. His pulse had become weak. He realized that Mehto's time had come. He could read the fear of death on his face. He called out gently, 'Mehto, how're you feeling?'

Mehto spoke as if awoken from sleep. 'I'm fine, brother. It's time to leave. Now you're Subhagi's father. I'm leaving her in your care.'

Sajan Singh replied, crying, 'Mehto, don't worry. God willing, you'll get well. I have always treated Subhagi as my daughter and shall continue to do so in future. Don't worry, so long as I am alive, no one would dare to trouble Lakshmi and Subhagi. You can say whatever you have on your mind.'

'I'll say no more. May God keep you ever prosperous.'

'Shall I call Ramu? You should forgive him for his follies.'

'No, brother. I don't want to see his face.'

After this, they began to prepare for *godaan* - the last sacred rite of offering a cow.

...

The whole village urged Ramu, but he refused to perform the last rites. He said, 'He refused to see my face at his deathbed. How can I regard myself as his son?'

Lakshmi lighted the funeral pyre. God knows how Subhagi had saved so much money, but when the preparations for the thirteenth day began, the villagers were astonished. Utensils, clothes, ghee, sugar – all these things were comfortably arranged. Ramu felt jealous that Subhagi was showing off in this way.

Lakshmi said, 'Beti, don't go beyond your means. There's no bread earner in the family. We have to live by whatever we can earn.'

Subhagi replied, 'Amma, we shall perform Babuji's thirteenth day rites with great pomp, whatever happens.

Babuji isn't going to come again. I want to show *bhayyia* what a woman can do. He must think that these two women can do nothing on their own. I want to put a dent in his pride.'

Lakshmi kept quiet. On the thirteenth day, brahmins from eight villages came to feast. Everyone applauded.

It was afternoon. People had feasted and gone away. Lakshmi, tired, had gone to sleep. Subhagi was winding up. Just then, Sajan Singh came in and asked her to take rest.

Subhagi said, 'Dada, I'm not tired. Have you added up? How much does it come to?'

'Beti, why do you ask?'

'No, I just want to know.'

'It must be about three hundred rupees.'

Subhagi said with hesitation, 'I owe this amount to you.'

'I won't ask you to pay. Mehto was my friend and brother. I too have some duty towards him.'

'It is enough that you have trusted me. Who would have lent me three hundred rupees?'

Sajan Singh marvelled at the wisdom this woman possessed.

...

Lakshmi's life felt like it had dried up after the death of her husband. Her loneliness after a fifty year long companionship looked like an uphill struggle. She felt that her mind, her bodily strength, her good sense – all had taken leave of her along with her dear husband.

Many a times, she prayed to God to take her life away too, but God did not accept this prayer. One has no control over one's death. Does it mean that one can't control one's life too?

Lakshmi, who was respected across the village for her wisdom, the one to whom people came for advice, was now a witless woman. She would not understand even the simplest of things.

From that very day, Lakshmi stopped eating. She would go to the kitchen on Subhagi's pleading, but she wouldn't eat anything. For fifty years, she had never eaten before her husband. How could she break this practice now?

She began to suffer coughing bouts, and soon became bed-ridden because of weakness. Subhagi was helpless. She had to work hard to pay back Thakur sahib's loan. Now her amma had fallen ill. If she went out, she had to leave her mother alone and if she stayed at home, she was not able to attend to her work in the field. Subhagi realized that the messengers of death had come for amma too. After all, dada also had the same kind of fever.

No one in the village had time to run about for her. Sajan Singh would call twice each day to see Lakshmi, to give her medicine and to advise Subhagi. However, Lakshmi's condition was deteriorating. She left the world fifteen days after her husband. During her last moments, Ramu came to touch her feet, but she rebuked him so hard that he could not come near her. She blessed Subhagi saying that she had found fulfilment in having such a daughter. She asked her to perform her last rites. She prayed to God that she should be born to her in her next life too.

...

After her mother's death, Subhagi had just one objective remaining in in life – to pay off Sajan Singh's debt. She had spent three hundred rupees on her father's funeral and now two hundred on her mother's. She had to pay off this debt of five hundred rupees all with her own effort. She did not lose courage. For three years, she worked day and night. People were astonished to see her working prowess and toughness. After attending to her fields during the day, she would grind four seers of flour at night. At the end of every month, she would go to Sajan Singh's house without fail to pay back fifteen rupees.

Now, she began to receive proposals for marriage. The villagers believed that whichever house she went to would be very fortunate. Subhagi, however, said that the day had not yet come.

She was wild with joy the day she paid off the last instalment of her debt. Her life's hardest trial had ended.

When she was about to go, Sajan Singh said to her, 'Beti, I have one request to make. Shall I? Promise that you won't refuse.'

Subhagi replied gratefully, 'Dada, who else should I obey, except you? I am so indebted to you.'

'If you have this feeling, then I won't say anything. I did not ask you because so far you had thought yourself indebted to me. Now you have cleared your debts. You are no longer under any obligation to me. Not a bit. Shall I ask?'

Subhagi said, 'What's your order?'

'Look, don't refuse. Otherwise, I shall never show my face to you.'

'Your order?'

'It's my wish that you should come to my house as my daughter-in-law. I used to believe in caste, but you have broken all my chains. My son worships you. You too have seen him. Do you accept?'

'Dada, I shall go mad receiving so much honour.'

'God himself is honouring you. You are an incarnation of goddess Bhagwati.'

'I regard you as my father. Whatever you do will be for my good. How can I refuse to obey your order?'

Sajan Singh put his hand on her head and said, 'Beti, may your husband live forever. You have accepted my proposal. No one can be more fortunate than me in this world.

• • •

GULLI-DANDA

Our urbanised friends may or may not agree, but I must say that gulli-danda is the king of all sports. Even today, whenever I see boys playing gulli-danda, I start rolling in delight and feel like joining them. There is no need of a lawn, or a shinguard, or a net, or a bat. Just cut a small branch from a tree and chip a small piece off it to make a gulli, and you begin to play even if you are just two people. The problem with more sophisticated games is that their kits are very expensive. For gulli-danda, you spend nothing, yet can have all the fun.

True, that a shot of gulli-danda can smash your eye. In the same way, a cricket ball can break your head, or damage your ligament, or crack your leg. Some of my sweetest memories are associated with this game. To come out early in the morning, to climb a tree to cut a few branches and chisel out the gullis and dandas, that excitement and involvement, those fights, that innocence in which differences between the touchable and untouchable, between the rich and the poor disappeared, where there was no room for pretension, or display of one's wealth, or pride – all this would be forgotten.

Among my playmates was a boy named Gaya. He was elder to me by two-three years - thin, tall, fingers like a monkey's, in appearance as well as their quickness and restlessness. The gulli might be of any shape, he pounced upon it like a lizard at an insect. I didn't know whether his parents were alive or where he lived or what he ate, but he was a champion player of our gulli-danda club. The team for which he played was sure to win. On seeing him come, we would dash towards him and urge him join our team.

One day, Gaya and I were playing. He was batting and I was fielding. Isn't it strange that we can enjoy batting the whole day, but don't like to field for even a minute. I tried all the tricks to wriggle out, but Gaya was not willing to let me go without completing his batting.

When my requests were of no avail, I deserted the field and ran homewards. Gaya ran after me and caught me. Flourishing the danda, he said, 'Go only after I have completed my batting. You were enjoying when I was fielding. How can you run away now when it is my turn to bat.'

'If you keep batting the whole day, should I keep on fielding?'

'Yes. You'll have to go on for the whole day.'

'And without food and water?'

'Yes, you can't go until I have had my turn.'

'Am I your slave?'

'Yes, you are.'

'I'm going home. Let me see how you stop me.'

'How can you go home? It's no joke. You have had your turn. Now, I must have mine.'

'Ok, yesterday gave you a guava to eat. Give it back to me.'

'That's gone into my tummy.'

'Take it out. Why did you eat it?'

'I ate it because you gave it to me. I didn't ask for it.'

'I won't field until you return my guava.'

I thought the justice was on my side. I must have given him that guava out of some selfish motive. No one does anything without self-interest. So if Gaya had eaten my guava, he had no right to ask me to field. People can suck your blood after bribing you, and this fellow has eaten my guava without wanting to give anything in return. I had bought five guavas for one paisa, which even Gaya's father wouldn't have been able to afford. He was being unjust through and through.

Gaya dragged me towards himself and said, 'I want my turn. I don't care about your guava or whatever.'

I had justice on my side, but he was bent upon being unjust. I wanted to run away, but he wouldn't let me go. I bit him with my teeth. He hit me with the danda. I started crying. Gaya couldn't stand against this weapon of mine and ran. I wiped my tears quickly and went home laughing. I, the son of a police station incharge, was beaten up by a lower caste boy! I felt humiliated, but I didn't talk about it to anyone at home.

...

Then, my father was transferred out. I was so thrilled at the idea of seeing the new place that I felt no regret at losing my companions. Father was unhappy. Here, the income was good. Mother was unhappy because everything was cheaper here, and she had become friendly with the neighbourhood women. But I was happy. I bragged about it to my friends. 'In the new city, the houses are different, touching the skies. There, if a teacher in an English medium school beat up a boy, he would be sent to jail.'

The wide-open eyes and wonderstruck faces of my friends told me how high I had gone up in their esteem.

The poor fellows were feeling envious of me and seemed to be saying. 'You are lucky, bhai. Go. We have to live and die in this wretched place.'

Twenty years passed by. I was an engineer now. I came to the same town for an inspection and stayed at the *dak* bungalow. My very presence in that place brought back the sweet memories of my childhood. I picked up my stick and came out to walk through the town. My eyes searched restlessly, like a thirsty traveller, for my childhood haunts, but nothing seemed familiar, except the name of the town.

Where there was a wasteland once, I found concrete houses. Where there was a banyan tree, I saw a beautiful park. Had I not known the name and the location, I wouldn't have recognized it. The undying memories of my childhood were opening their arms to meet my old friends, but this world had changed. I longed to see its old face.

All of a sudden, I saw two-three boys playing gulli-danda in an open space. For a moment, I forgot who I was - a big officer, with my officer-ship, power and authority in full show.

I went close to them and asked a boy, 'Son, does a man by the name of Gaya live here?'

One of the boys answered, somewhat overawed, 'Gaya? Gaya, the *chamar*?'

I said, 'Yes, yes, the same.'

'Yes, there is.'

'Can you call him?'

The boy ran away, and in a short while, I saw him coming back accompanied by a dark, gigantic man. I recognized him from a distance and wanted to take him in my embrace at once, but stopped for some reason. I said, 'Gaya, do you recognize me?'

Gaya bowed down to salute me. 'Yes, *malik*. Why wouldn't I ? How have you been?'

'Oh fine. And you?'

'I'm the deputy sahib's syce.'

'Where're Mattai, Durga and Mohan? Do you have any news about them?'

'Mattai's dead. Durga and Mohan have become postmen. And you?'

'I'm the district engineer.'

'Sarkar, you were always very bright.'

'Do you ever play gulli-danda anymore?'

Gaya looked at me with surprise, 'How can I play, sarkar? I get no time off.'

'Come, let's play today. You bat. I'll field. I owe you a turn. You can square it today.'

Gaya agreed only after great persuasion. He was a petty labourer. I, a big officer. There was no match. He was feeling embarrassed. So was I. Not because I was playing against Gaya, but because I felt that people would treat this as a great tamasha and assemble in a big crowd. But I couldn't resist the temptation to play. We decided to go and play far away from the habitation. No one would be there to watch us and we would be able to relive the sweet memories of our childhood. I brought Gaya back to the *dak* bungalow and both of us drove to an open spot. We had carried an axe too. I was treating it as fun, but Gaya had become very serious about it. There was no trace of excitement or pleasure on his face. Perhaps he was lost in thinking about the divide that now existed between us.

I asked, 'Gaya, tell me honestly, did you ever think of me?'

Gaya replied, somewhat bashfully, 'How should I remember you, *hazoor*? I'm worth nothing. It was my good luck to play with you for a few days. That's all.'

I said, saddened a bit, 'But I always remembered you. Your danda, with which you beat me up so hard. Don't you remember it?'

'That was out of boyishness. Don't remind me of that, sarkar.'

'What! That's the best memory of my childhood. The enjoyment that I get remembering that incident, I find nowhere; neither in the respect I get, nor in the money I have. There was something in that which is still sweet.'

By this time, we had driven nearly three miles away from the town. There was silence all around. Towards the west was the marshland spreading for miles across. I quickly climbed up a tree and came down after cutting a branch. A gulli and danda were ready in no time.

The game began. I positioned the gulli over the small boat-shaped hole, the starting point, and struck it with the danda. The gulli flew right in front of Gaya. He raised his hand as if to catch a fish, but the gulli fell just behind him. It was the same Gaya in whose hands the gulli would land as if of its own will, or as if by some magnetic power.

But today, the gulli showed no love for him. Then, I sent him on a gulli chase. I broke all the rules, substituting cheating for my lack of practice. I kept on playing even when I had missed hitting the gulli, though according to the rules, it should have been Gaya's turn to bat. Whenever I failed to drive the gulli far, I ran to pick it up myself and started again. Gaya was watching all these violations, but he said nothing, as if he had forgotten all the rules.

His aim had been so perfect that the gulli would always hit the danda with a clatter. The gulli's only purpose after release from his hand was to hit the danda. But today, it refused. It went either left or right or fell short, or went across.

After he had fielded for half an hour, the gulli hit the danda, but I cheated, saying that it hadn't.

Gaya didn't protest.

'It might have missed.'

'Had it hit, I won't have denied.'

'No, bhaiya, why should you lie?'

During our childhood, he wouldn't have spared my life had I cheated like this. He would have caught me by the neck. But today, I was cheating so openly. The donkey! He had forgotten everything.

Suddenly, the gulli hit the danda like a bullet. Against this clear proof that I couldn't cheat, I thought of changing the truth into falsehood once again. What would I lose? If he agreed, it would be great, but if he didn't, there was no harm in fielding for a while. I'll wriggle out, appealing for bad light.

Gaya shouted in a victorious mood, 'It has hit! It has hit! With a loud clatter.'

I pretended. 'Did you see it hit? I didn't.'

'It made a clattering noise, sarkar.'

'It might have hit a brick.'

It surprised me how such a sentence could have come out of my mouth. To turn this truth into falsehood was like calling the day night. Both of us had seen the gulli hit the danda, yet Gaya accepted my version.

'Yes, it must have hit a brick. Had it hit the danda, it wouldn't have made such a clattering noise.'

I began to bat again. But after such blatant cheating, I began to pity Gaya's naivety. When the gulli hit the danda a third time, I agreed to field out of generosity.

Gaya said, 'Now it's dark, bhaiya, let's play tomorrow.'

I thought for a moment, 'Tomorrow he will have too much time and God knows for how long he will make me field. It is better to call it quits today itself.'

'No, no. There's plenty of light. You take your turn.'

'We won't be able to see the gulli.'

'Don't worry.'

Gaya started batting, but he was terribly out of practice. He tried to strike the gulli twice, but failed each time. His turn was over in less than a minute. I tried to be generous.

'You can have another turn. You have missed your very first shot,' I said.

'No, bhaiya, it's already dark.'

'You're out of practice. Don't you play now?'

'There's no time, bhaiya.'

Both of us got into the car and were back in town before darkness. As he was going away, Gaya said to me, 'Tomorrow there is a match here. All the old players would come. Would you come? I'll call them when you are free.'

I agreed and went there in the evening to watch the match the next day. There were ten players in all. Some of them were my boyhood companions. A majority of the players were young, whom I did not know. The match began. I watched sitting inside my car. Today, I was astonished to see Gaya's skill. When he struck the gulli, it flew into the sky. There was no trace of the previous day's hesitation or lack of interest. Had he made me field like this, I would have cried. The gulli travelled two hundred yards when he struck it with his danda.

One of the fielders tried to cheat. Gaya caught him and they were about to come to blows, but the young boy backed out when he saw Gaya's face flushed with anger. Had he not backed out, there would have been a fight. I was not playing, yet I was enjoying it all, reminded of the good old days of boyhood. Now I realized that the previous day, Gaya had only pretended to be playing. He had taken pity on me. I had cheated, but he didn't lose his temper, because he was not really playing. He was only kidding with me. He didn't want to torture me by making me chase the gulli endlessly.

I was an officer and this officer-ship had become a wall between us. Now, I could get his respect, but not his companionship. During our boyhood, we were equals. There was no distance between us. But now in this position, I was an object of his pity. He didn't recognize me as his equal. He had grown taller and I had grown smaller.

DO BAILON KI KATHA

THE TALE OF TWO BULLOCKS

Jhuri, the vegetable farmer, had two bullocks named Hira and Moti. Both were of fine Pachai stock, of great stature, beautiful to behold, and diligent at their labours. The two had lived together for a very long time and become sworn brothers. Face to face or side by side they would hold discussions in their silent language. How each understood the other's thoughts we cannot say, but they certainly possessed some mysterious power. They would express their love by licking and sniffing one another, and sometimes they would even lock horns – not from hostility but rather out of friendship and a sense of fun, any friendship lacking such displays seems rather superficial and insipid and not to be trusted. When the oilseed cake and straw was tossed into the manager they would stand up together, thrust their muzzles in to the trough together, and sit down side by side. When one withdrew his mouth the other would do so too.

On one occasion, Jhuri sent the pair to his father-in-law's. How could the bullocks know why they were being sent away? They assumed that the master had sold them. If God had given them speech, they would have asked Jhuri, 'Why are you throwing us poor wretches out! We've done everything possible to serve you well. If working as hard as we did couldn't get the job done, you could have made us work still harder. We were willing to die labouring for you. We never complained about the food, whatever you gave us to eat we bowed our heads and ate it, so why did you sell us into the hands of this tyrant?'

At evening, the two bullocks reached their new place, hungry after a whole day without food, but when they were brought to the manger, neither even stuck his mouth in. Their hearts were heavy; they were separated from the home they had thought was their own. New house, new village, new people, all seemed alien to them.

They consulted in their mute language, glancing at one another out of the corners of their eyes, and lay down. When the village was deep in sleep the two of them pulled hard, broke their yoke together and set out for home. That tether was very tough, no one could have guessed that any bullock could break it; but a redoubled power had entered into them and the ropes snapped with one violent jerk.

When he got up early in the morning, Jhuri saw that his two bullocks were standing at the trough, half a tether dangling from each of their necks. Their legs were muddled up to the knees and resentful love gleamed in their eyes.

When Jhuri saw the bullocks, he was overwhelmed with affection for them. He ran and threw his arms around their necks, and very pleasant was the spectacle of that loving embrace.

The children of the household and the village boys gathered, clapping their hands in welcome.

One boy said, 'Nobody has bullocks like these,' and another agreed, 'They came back from so far all by themselves,' while a third said, 'They're not bullocks, in an earlier life they were men,' and nobody dared to disagree with this.

When Jhuri's wife saw the bullocks at the gate, she got angry and said, 'What loafers these oxen are! They didn't work at my father's place for one day before they ran away!'

Jhuri could not listen to his bullocks being slandered like this. 'Loafers, are they? At your father's, they must not have fed them. What were they to do?'

Aggravated, she said, 'They ran away just because those people don't make fools of themselves spoiling them like you. They feed them but they also make them work hard. These two are real lazy-bones and they ran away. Let's see them get oilseed and bran now? I'll give them nothing but dry straw, they can eat it or drop dead.'

So it came about. The hired hand was given strict orders to feed them nothing but dry straw.

When the bullocks put their faces in the trough they found it insipid. No savour, no juice--how could they eat it? With eyes full of hope, they began to stare toward the door.

Jhuri said to the hired hand, 'Why the devil don't you throw in a little oilseed?'

'The mistress would surely kill me.'

'Then do it on the sly.'

'Oh no, boss. Afterwards, you'll side with her.'

The next day, Jhuri's brother-in-law, Gaya, came back again and took the bullocks away. This time, he yoked them to the wagon. Moti tried to knock the wagon into the ditch a couple of times, but Hira, who was more tolerant, held him back.

When they reached the house, Gaya tied them with thick ropes. Again, he threw down the same dry straw. But to his own bullocks he gave oilseed cake, ground lentils, everything.

The two bullocks had never suffered such an insult. Jhuri wouldn't strike them even with a newer stem. The two of them would rise up at a click of his tongue, while here they were beaten. Along with the pain of injured pride, they had to put up with dry straw. They didn't even bother to look in the trough.

The next day, Gaya yoked them to the plow, but it was as though the two of them had sworn an oath not to lift a foot. He grew tired beating them but not one foot would they lift. One time, when the cruel fellow delivered a sharp blow on Hira's nostrils, Moti's anger went out of control and he took to his heels with the plow. Plough-share, rope, yoke, harness, all were smashed to pieces. Had there not been strong ropes around their necks, it would have been impossible to catch the two of them.

Hira said in his silent language, 'Its useless to run away.'

Moti answered, 'But he was going to kill you.'

'We'll really get beaten now.'

'So what? We were born bullocks, how can we escape beating!?'

'Gaya's coming on the run with a couple of men and they're all carrying sticks.'

Moti said, 'Just say the word and I'll show them a little fun. Here he comes with his stick!'

'No, brother!' Hira cautioned. 'Just stand still.' 'If he beats me, I'll knock one or two of them down.' 'No, that's not the dharma of our community.'

Moti could only stand, protesting violently in his heart. Gaya arrived, caught them and took them away. Fortunately, he didn't beat them this time, for if he had, Moti would have struck back.

Again the same dry straw was brought to them that day. They stood in silence. In the house, the people were eating dinner. Just then, a quite young girl came out carrying a couple of pieces of bread. She fed the two of them and went away. How could a piece of bread still their hunger? But in their hearts, they felt as though they had been fed a full meal. Here too was the dwelling of some gentle folk. The girl was Bharo's daughter; her mother was dead and her stepmother beat her often, so she felt a kind of sympathy for the bullocks.

The two were yoked all day, took a lot of beatings, and got stubborn. In the evening, they were tied up in their stall, and at night, the same little girl would come out and feed some bread to each of them. The happy result of this communion of love was that even though they ate only a few mouthfuls of the dry straw, they did not grow weak; their eyes and every cell of their bodies was still full of rebelliousness.

One day, Moti said in his silent language, 'I can't stand it any longer, Hira. What do you say, tonight we'll break the ropes and run away!'

'Yes, I'll agree to that, but how can we break such a thick rope!'

'There is a way. First gnaw the rope' a bit, then it will snap with one jerk.'

At night, when the girl had fed them and gone off, the two began to gnaw at their ropes, but the thick cord wouldn't fit in their mouths. The poor fellows tried hard over and over again, but without any luck. Suddenly, the door of the house opened and the same girl came out. The bullocks lowered their heads and began to lick her hand. Their tails stood up while she stroked their foreheads, and then she said, 'I'm going to let you go. Be very quiet and run away or these people will kill you. In the house today, they were talking about putting rings in your noses.'

She untied the rope, but the two stood silent.

'Well, let's go,' said Hira, 'Only tomorrow, this orphan's going to be in a lot of trouble. Everybody in the house will suspect her.'

Suddenly the girl yelled, 'Uncle's bullocks are running away! Daddy, daddy, come quick, they're running away!'

Gaya came rushing out of the house to catch the bullocks. They were running now, with Gaya fast behind them. They ran even faster and Gaya set up a shout. He then turned back to fetch some men of the village. This was the chance for the two friends to make their escape, and they ran straight ahead, no longer aware of where they were. There was no trace of the familiar road they'd come by. Then the two of them halted at the edge of a field and began to think about what they ought to do now.

Hira said, 'It appears we've lost our way.'

'You took to your heels without thinking. We should have knocked him down dead right on the spot.'

'If we'd killed him, what would the world say? He abandoned his dharma, but we stuck to ours.'

They were dizzy with hunger. Peas were growing in the field and they began to browse, stopping occasionally to listen for anyone coming.

They had scarcely eaten a couple of mouthfuls when two men with sticks came running and surrounded the two friends. Hira was on the embankment and slipped away, but Moti was down in the soggy field. His hooves were so deep in mud that he couldn't run, and was caught. When Hira saw his comrade in trouble he dashed back. If they were going to be trapped, then they'd be trapped together. The watchmen caught him too.

Early in the morning, the two friends were shut up in a village pound. The two friends stayed tied up there for a week. No one gave them so much as a bit of hay. True, water was given to them once. This was all their nourishment. They got so weak that they could not even stand up, and their ribs were sticking out. One day, someone beat a drum outside the enclosure and towards noon, about fifty or sixty people gathered there. The two friends were brought out and the inspection began. People came and studied their appearance and went away disappointed. Who would buy bullocks that looked like corpses!

Suddenly, there came a bearded man with red eyes and a cruel face. He began to talk with the clerk. When they saw his expression, the hearts of the two friends grew weak from what their intuition told them. They had no doubt at all as to who he was and why he had his eyes on them. They looked at one another with frightened eyes and lowered their heads.

Hira said, 'We ran away from Gaya's house in vain. We won't survive this.'

Without much faith, Moti answered, 'They say God has mercy on everybody. Why isn't He being merciful to us?'

'To God, it's all the same whether we live or die. Don't worry, it's not so bad. We'll be with Him in a little while. Once He saved us in the shape of that little girl, so won't He save us now."

'This man is going to cut our throats. Just watch.'

'So, why worry! Every bit of us, flesh, hide, horns and bones, will be used for something or the other.

When the auction was over, the friends went off with that bearded man. Every bit of their bodies was trembling. They could scarcely lift their feet, but they were so frightened they managed to keep stumbling along--for if they slowed down the least bit, they'd get a good whack from the stick.

Along the way, they saw a herd of cows and bullocks grazing in a verdant meadow. All the animals were happy, sleek and supple. Some were leaping about, others lying down contentedly chewing their cud. What a happy life was theirs! Yet how selfish they all were. Not one of them cared about how their two brothers must be suffering after falling into the hands of the butcher.

Suddenly, it seemed to them that the road was familiar. Yes, this was the road by which Gaya had taken them away. They were coming to the same fields and orchards, the same villages. At every instant, their pace quickened. All their fatigue and weariness disappeared. Oh, just look, here was their own meadow, here was the same well where they had worked the winch to pull up the bucket, yes, it was the same well.

Moti said, ‘Our house is close by!' 'It's God's mercy!' said Hira. 'As for me, I'm making a run for home!'

'Will he let us go?’

'I’ll knock him down and kill him.’

'No, no, run and make it to our stalls. We won't budge from there.'

As though they'd gone crazy, joyfully kicking up their heels like calves, they made off for the house. There was their stall! They ran and stood by it while the bearded man came dashing after them.

Jhuri was sitting in his doorway sunning himself. As soon as he saw the bullocks, he ran and embraced them over and over again. Tears of joy flowed from the two friends' eyes, and one of them licked Jhuri's hand.

The bearded man came up and grabbed their tethers. 'These are my bullocks,' said Jhuri.

'How can they be! I just bought them at an auction at the cattle pound.'

'I bet you stole them,' said Jhuri. 'Just shut up and leave. They're my bullocks. They'll be sold only when I sell them. Who has the right to auction off my bullocks?'

The bearded man said, 'I'll go to the police station and make a complaint.'

'They're my bullocks. The proof is that they came and stood at my door.'

In a rage, the bearded man stepped forward to drag the bullocks away. This is when Moti lowered his horns. The bearded man stepped back. Moti charged and the man took to his heels with Moti after him, and stopped only at the outskirts of the village where he took his stand guarding the road. The butcher stopped at some distance, yelled back threats and insults and threw scenes. Moti stood blocking his path like a victorious hero. The villagers came out to watch the entertainment and had a good laugh. When the bearded man acknowledged defeat and went away, Moti came back strutting.

Hira said, 'I was afraid you'd get so mad that you'd go and kill him.'

'If he'd caught me, I wouldn't have given up before I'd killed him.'

'Won't he come back now?'

'If he does, I'll take care of him long before he gets here.'

'What if he has us shot?'

'Then I'll be dead, but I'll be of no use to him.'

'Nobody thinks of the life we have as being a life.'

'Only because we're so simple.'

In a little while, their trough was filled with oilseed cake, hay, bran and grain, and the two friends began to eat. Jhuri stood by and stroked them, while a dozen boys watched the show.

Excitement seemed to have spread through the whole village.

At this moment, the mistress of the house came out and kissed each of the bullocks on the forehead.

THAKUR KA KUAN

THAKUR'S WELL

Jhokhu brought the lota to his mouth, but the water smelled foul. He said to Gangi, 'What kind of water is this? It stinks so much, I can't drink it! My throat's burning and you give me water that's turned bad.'

Every evening, Gangi filled the water jugs. The well was a long way off and it was hard for her to make several trips. She'd brought this water the previous day and there'd been no bad smell at all. How could it be there now? She lifted the lota to her nostrils and it certainly smelt foul. Surely, some animal must have fallen into the well and died. She didn't know where else she could get any water.

No one would let her walk up to the Thakur's well. Even when she was at a distance from it, people would start yelling at her. At the other end of the village, the shopkeeper had a well, but even there they wouldn't let her draw water. For people like herself, there wasn't any well in the village.

Jhokhu, who'd been sick for several days, held back his thirst for a little while. Then he said, 'I'm so thirsty, I can't stand it. Bring me the water, I'll hold my nose and drink a little.

Gangi did not give it to him. His sickness would get worse from drinking bad water, that much she knew. She didn't know, however, that by boiling the water, it could be made safe. She said, ‘How can you drink it? Who knows what kind of beast has died in it! I'll go and get you some water from the well.'

Surprised, Jokhu stared at her. 'Where will you get more water?'

'The Thakur and the shopkeeper both have wells. Won't they let me fill just one lota?’

'You'll come back with your arms and legs broken, that's all. You'd better just sit down and keep quiet. The Brahman will give a curse, the Thakur will beat you with a stick, and that money-lending shopkeeper takes five for every bowl-full he gives. Do you think people like that are going to let you draw water from their wells?’ Gangi could not deny the truth in these harsh words, but she couldn't let him drink that stinking water.

By nine that night, Gangi reached the Thakur's property to get water from his well.

The dim glow of a small oil lamp had lit up the well. Gangi sat hidden behind the wall and began to wait for the right moment. Everybody in the village drank water from his well. It was closed to nobody. Only those unlucky ones like herself could not use their buckets here.

Gangi suddenly felt very angry. Why was she so low and those others so high! Just because they wore a thread around their necks? There wasn't one of them in the village who wasn't rotten. They stole, they cheated, they lied in court, then how were they so high and mighty?

She heard people approaching the well and her heart began to pound. If anybody saw her, she'd get an awful kicking out of it. She grabbed her bucket and rope and crept away to hide in the dark shadows of a tree.

Two women had come to draw water and they were talking. One said, ‘There they were eating and they order us to get more water.'

'You'll never see them pick up the pitcher and fetch it themselves.’

After they had filled their buckets and left, Gangi came out from the shadows of the tree and drew close to the well platform. The idlers had left, the Thakur had shut his door and gone inside to the courtyard to sleep. Gangi took a moment to sigh with relief. On every side, the field was clear. Gangi tiptoed up on to the well platform. Never before had she felt such a sense of triumph.

She looped the rope around the bucket. Like some soldier stealing into the enemy's fortress at night, she peered cautiously on every side. If she were caught now, the slightest hope of mercy or leniency won't be there. Finally, with a prayer to the Gods, she mustered up her courage and cast the bucket into the well.

Slowly, it sank in the water. There was not the slightest sound. Gangi yanked it back up with all her might to the rim of the well. No strong-armed athlete could have dragged it up more swiftly.

She had just stooped to catch it and set it on the wall when suddenly, the Thakur's door opened. The jaws of a tiger could not have terrified her more.

The rope escaped from her hand. With a crash, the bucket fell into the water, the rope after it. For a few seconds after, there were sounds of splashing inside.

Yelling 'Who's there' Who's there?' the Thakur came toward the well. Gangi jumped from the platform and ran way as fast as she could. When she reached home, Jokhu, with the lota at his mouth, was drinking that filthy, stinking water.

• • •

Printed by Libri Plureos GmbH in Hamburg, Germany